Wasim
AND THE
CHAMP

For my family – *us* – C.A.

Text copyright © Chris Ashley 2011
Illustrations copyright © Kate Pankhurst 2011
The right of Chris Ashley to be identified as the author and of Kate Pankhurst
to be identified as the illustrator of this work has been asserted by them in accordance
with the Copyright, Designs and Patents Act, 1988 (United Kingdom).

First published in Great Britain in 2011 by
Frances Lincoln Children's Books, 4 Torriano Mews,
Torriano Avenue, London NW5 2RZ
www.franceslincoln.com

A catalogue record for this book is available from the British Library.

ISBN 978-1-84780-057-2

Set in Garamond

Printed in Croydon, Surrey, UK by CPI Bookmarque Ltd. in January 2011

1 3 5 7 9 8 6 4 2

Wasim
AND THE
CHAMP

Chris Ashley

Illustrated by Kate Pankhurst

F

FRANCES LINCOLN
CHILDREN'S BOOKS

Chapter One

First in. First out. First in the line. Wasim was always first. "First, worst!" the other children used to shout, but they knew Wasim didn't listen, so they'd given up. It was what he did. Wasim was always first.

And he was first tonight – Monday – after prayers. His *topi* prayer cap was on his head, his trainers were back on his feet, he had his Koran and he was at the door.

He turned to see if Atif – or, even better,

Faizhan – had tried to beat him and. . .

"STOP!"

Wasim's hand snapped back as if a million volts of electricity had buzzed through the old wooden door handle.

"Stop." The voice was calm again, back to Uncle Zan's normal voice. "Wasim, *khush karna* . . . please."

Wasim just stood, his mouth open. He had never heard that shout before. Uncle Zan was normally a quiet man.

"There are . . . there are *people* outside."

Silence. The shout had shocked everybody gathered in the entrance to the mosque, where piles of shoes sat and joined in the stillness.

One second . . . two. . . And then there was silence no more, stillness no more.

The window by the door shattered with

a splintering clatter. There was a thud, as half
a brick crumbled high against the wall and
then plopped down onto a pair of shiny
black shoes. There were screams from
children and shouts from grown-ups and
then a snarling face, ugly with hate, shouting
the P word through the broken window. A
fizzing sound and a smell of bonfire night...

"Go! Go!" People scrambled back to the
chants of the prayer hall as the screams
and the fizzing got louder and the smoke
in the small entrance to the mosque turned
more and more blue. Wasim couldn't move.
He hadn't even breathed since Uncle Zan's
shout, and his hand was still shaking by the
door handle.

When he finally did breathe, smoke
tore at the back of his throat and made
him choke. Dad was striding towards him,

eyes wide, arms stretched, ready to yank him away, but Wasim's watering eyes were on Uncle Zan. *Zan's* eyes were calm, and they met Wasim's with a sad smile. And then the old man bent into the smoke, picked up the firework and dropped it out of the broken window. He nodded Wasim away from the door and stood there as men in shalwar kameez shirts and blazing youths in Adidas tops bundled towards it, ready for battle with the hate-mob outside.

Uncle Zan shook his head and herded them all towards the madrasa classroom, where only a few minutes ago, Wasim had been learning. Shouts of blazing anger beat against the door from the inside and bottles and stones battered it from outside. But nobody passed Uncle Zan. Gradually the smoke cleared and so did the entrance hall,

and the distant shouts and howls from
outside were replaced by the sound of
a police siren. There were running feet
and the barks of dogs.

It was over...

For tonight.

Chapter Two

They all stayed together once they were
back home. Shamaila was still crying, so
she was allowed to stay in the front room
with the TV.

The news was still all about London.
There had been an explosion the day before
and the screen was filled with smoke and
sirens and people sweeping up glass. Mum
shook her head and met Dad's eyes.

And then it showed more glass and
there were different policemen. But this time
not because of an explosion. There was a
minaret, the domed tower of a mosque,
in the background . . . and there were
teenagers in hoodies.

"That's us, that's us!" shouted Shamaila
from Mum's knee. Wasim remembered the
walk to the car past the slouched shoulders
and finger signs, baseball caps and hoodies.
They had all sloped away once the police
dogs got there.

Atif, Wasim's brother, answered.
"No. That's a different mosque. . . It's
because of what happened in London."

Then there were different minarets,
different hoodies and a different newsman
speaking to the camera. It was happening
everywhere.

Wasim spoke for the first time since the mosque. "What? They think the explosion was us? Is that why they threw stuff?" He could still taste the firework smoke catching at his throat.

Dad snorted a not-funny laugh. "*They* don't think, Wasim. *They* know we are Muslim and so they throw stones at a mosque where we worship. *They* don't know you or me, Uncle Zan, Mum, Atif or Shamaila, or the millions from our faith who are shocked and angry at that explosion. *They* don't know us, just like whoever made that explosion didn't know the people they could have hurt. *They* don't think either."

Wasim was quiet then. The news went on to a story about a singing dog that made Shamaila laugh, so finally she could go up to bed.

"Will more people throw things at us?" she asked.

Dad shook his head as he went into the kitchen. "No, they don't know us," he said.

Then it was just Atif and Wasim.

"They do know us," said Atif. "That lad who threw the firework goes to my school."

Wasim nodded. He'd seen them too. His eyes had met Jason Coolley's from under his hood . . . and Lee Raynor's. They'd left last year or the year before, and now they were at High School. But they knew Wasim. And Wasim knew them.

⊙ ⊙ ⊙

Morning. Twenty past eight. Wasim and Atif waited at the door. They always left at twenty past. Dave and Andy from down the road

knocked for them and that gave Atif
time to get the bus for the High School
and Wasim time for the first footie game
of the day in the playground at his school.

Twenty-two minutes past. No Dave
or Andy. Atif checked his phone.

Twenty-three minutes past.

Twenty-four minutes past. The bus for
the high school went at half past from the
main road.

Twenty-five past. They opened the door
and shouted a goodbye back to Mum, who
was helping Shamaila into her uniform.

"Got your lunch? Where is David?
And Andrew?"

The boys looked at each other.

At twenty-six minutes past they left.

Atif had to sprint and Wasim kept up,
his rucksack banging on his back and forcing

his glasses down his nose. They clattered down the hill and round the corner onto the main road, and there was the bus moving off.

Atif slowed down and half waved to stop it but the bus carried on, picking up speed, and the bus driver pretended not to see him. . . And so did Dave and Andy sitting in the front seats.

But Jason Coolley, Lee Raynor and a bundle of romping mates at the back window had seen them. The finger

signs and fists showed that.

Wasim watched his brother's shoulders slump as he made his way slowly back to the bus stop. He would be late now. Detention. Plus his 100 per cent punctuality record would be gone. But Wasim knew that wasn't what was hurting Atif. The pretending-not-to-see eyes of Dave and Andy hurt more than the bricks and bottles from last night could have done.

"What are *we* supposed to have done?" Atif mumbled as he read the timetable on the bus stop. "See you later," he added, "the next one's at ten to. . ."

Wasim hesitated. He thought of missing his morning footie, and of the day starting with Numeracy instead of a playground match, and of getting a late-person's glare from Mrs Slocombe, the secretary.

"I'll wait with you," he said.

Atif's sad eyes managed a smile.

"Chewy?" He reached into his pocket and the two brothers chewed gum together in silence until the long, double-jointed bus hissed round the corner and they went to face their separate Ahmed days.

Chapter Three

They were just lining up in the playground when Wasim got there, so he wasn't too late. Wasim felt the heaviness in his chest ease off a bit as he got back to school and the normal world. The world before the bomb in London had started what Dad called the 'situation'.

He felt even better when he ran past the railings and saw the banner being tied to

them by Mrs Caulfield, the caretaker. Summer
Fun Day. Saturday was the Fun Day – helping
on a stall, games, pony rides on the field,
beating the goalie and the six-a-side
tournament. The Super Sixes. A tournament
with a proper cup and, Mr Abbott said,
medals. Lists of teams had to be in by
Wednesday.

And it wasn't just from their school.

Teams from all over the town would be playing.

The line trooped in and Wasim joined the end.

Their team was almost ready – Rock Star Rovers. It was Wasim, Charles and Gary from their school, Atif, Andy and Dave from the High School. They had already sorted out what colours they were going to play in and they'd been training at the park.

"Wasim!"

"Wasim!"

"Planet Earth to Wasim Ahmed!"

"Here, Miss!" Wasim looked up from the mess of crumpled worksheets, forgotten newsletters and broken pencils that were stuffed into his tray.

Mrs Scott was cross. "That was the third time, Wasim. What is so important that you are not learning your Look/Cover/Write/ Check spellings? Oh, I might have known. . ."

He'd found it. It was crumpled but it was in his hands – the entry form for the six-a-side tournament. He had to make sure that Rock Star Rovers's entry was handed in today.

"I'll take that, young man. There is work to do this week before the summer fair takes over."

"But, but. . ." But there was no but-ing Mrs Scott once she'd decided, and now the entry form was on her desk.

"You can collect this tomorrow, Wasim.

Once I've seen how much work you manage today."

Wasim pretended to look, cover, write and check his spellings, but he was thinking.

Charles would have a form. They still needed one more player, maybe two if they were going to have a sub. Joe? No, he didn't like football. Gemma? She was good, but she was doing the face painting and didn't want to be in it. Todd? No, he'd said he wouldn't give a pound to play, they should pay him. Dionne? He was already in Ben's team. Faizhan from the mosque? Wasim hadn't seen him play and he didn't like him, anyway, because he showed off about how quickly he learned the Koran. He reckoned he was good at football, but then Faizhan reckoned he was good at everything.

Wasim lined up for assembly and then sat and tried to catch Charles's eye to do their secret *honk honk* noise and flipper-clapping because Mr Abbott had said that it was going to be a SEAL assembly about everybody living together in the world as friends.

But Wasim got caught, so he had to spend playtime doing lines – *SEAL means the social and emotional aspects of learning* – when he should have been getting an extra player for Rock Star Rovers. And it was another football playtime missed. Two in one day!

Atif would have to get another player from his school. Anyway, it would be better to have another older kid. They'd stand more chance of winning.

SEAL means the social and emotional aspects of learning.

Honk Honk flapped Charles with his seal flippers, passing by with the milk for Junior S.

⊙ ⊙ ⊙

Back at home, though, Rock Star Rovers was not on Atif's mind. It didn't seem like anything was. The front door had crashed shut. There was the thud of his bag hitting the hall floor and then the sound of him banging up the stairs.

"Atif, Atif. . ." Shamaila had a picture from school to show him, but another bang from upstairs meant that the bathroom door had been shut and the lock was on.

Wasim didn't budge from the settee where he was watching *Mynotaur Man*, but just shouted, "Atif, we need another player."

There was no answer. Wasim waited to see if Mynotaur would defeat the extraterrestrial dinosaur that was screeching from the TV.

Once Mynotaur had won and the earth was safe once again, Wasim yawned his way upstairs and into the bedroom. He flung himself onto the bed with a double bounce.

"We need another player," he said to the hump in Atif's blankets. "Another player, Atif. Atif?"

Wasim sat up. Something was wrong. Usually he would have had to fight to watch the end of *Mynotaur Man* because Atif would have tried to change the channel. And bouncing on the bed like Wasim had just done could get them grounded, so on any other night, Atif would have had a go at him.

Wasim leant across the gap between their

beds and pulled back the blanket. His brother was lying curled up, his chin on his chest.

"Go away," Atif whispered and he grabbed at the blanket.

Wasim pulled it again. This time Atif turned and Wasim dodged back, expecting a playful slap. But it didn't come. Instead, Wasim saw his brother's face and he felt sick.

"What happened. . .? Who. . .? Mum! Dad!"

Atif was a state. One eye was closed and red and there was a blue mark growing on his ballooning cheek. His lip was massive and there was a big split where a tooth had smashed through.

"Who did it?"

Mum came up the stairs to answer Wasim's shout. She just gasped and held her face when she saw Atif. Then she held *his* face and Wasim could see how hard his brother was working not to cry as he struggled away and stood up in the now crowded bedroom.

"Who did it?"

"I dunno," was all Atif would mumble. "Loads of us got hit. . . And loads of them by the end."

"Us?" Mum asked. "Them?"

And Wasim remembered the kids on the bus and knew what Atif meant.

And then he remembered how down his brother had looked that morning and how he, Wasim, had then gone into school and only had to worry about spellings and finding a player and whether anyone would laugh at his SEAL joke.

But Atif had gone into his school, his best friends blanking him, and had been hurt with fists or feet, because . . . because of a madman in London, the colour of his skin and the place where he prayed.

Atif wouldn't say much at all after that. He said again that he didn't know who had hit him. He had been lining up at the tuck shop. There had been lots of trouble in his school. He knew why.

Everybody knew why. 'The Situation.'

Mum bathed his swollen face and Dad, when he came in, bit his own fist with anger.

"I'm going to that school now. I'll find them."

This time it was Mum who did the calming.

"Atif says he doesn't know who did it. And this is just what they want, the people who spoil things. The people who don't want us all in this town, living together."

Dad listened. But there were tooth marks in his fists by the time Uncle Zan arrived with a kind wink and a ruffle of the hair for Atif and his usual joke with Shamaila.

Then he was in the front room with Dad and other people Wasim recognised from the mosque, and the door was shut.

Chapter Four

Wasim was allowed out, but only as far as the garages. He started booting his ball against the door that was usually the United home goal, but his heart wasn't in it. He hardly made it clang loudly enough to get shouted at by the woman in the bottom flat who moaned about everything, or to get a clap from Mr Holloway who always came out to watch when there was no horse racing on TV.

Wasim kicked a stone instead, and then had his first happy moment of the day when Mr Holloway appeared on his balcony and made his cup of tea sign. He did this by miming tipping up a cup with his little finger sticking out. It always made Wasim laugh, and usually meant a cup of milky tea in a mug with a picture of an old king on it, and sometimes a Jammie Dodger biscuit.

"Coming aboard?"

Mr Holloway used to sail ships all over the world and he had even been to Karachi, where Wasim's Dad had been born. He had a story about everyone and everything and Wasim loved spending time with him.

'Coming aboard' meant climbing up a dustbin onto the corner garage roof and balancing along the concrete edge of the garages (you would fall through if you went

in the middle). Then you had to grab Mr Holloway's shaking hand and climb over the railing of his balcony. It was almost as much fun as the football they played down below. Today, though, Wasim just shrugged and climbed up without his usual battle to keep the smile from his face.

"Come aboard, matey. You ready for some rations?"

Wasim sat in the deckchair that overlooked his football pitch – the garages – and felt the great weight in his chest again. They should have been training down there tonight, getting ready to win the Super Sixes. Now Atif was silent and bruised at home and everyone was against them, the Ahmeds . . . the Muslims.

"Get yer laughing gear round that, and then tell old Hollow Legs what's bothering you." 'Hollow legs' was what they used to call him at sea, Mr Holloway said. "And don't tell me nothing's up. I've never seen you without a smile on that old mug of yours before."

Mr Holloway plonked a cup of milky tea and a Penguin bar in front of Wasim. The old eyes that had been everywhere and seen everything searched into Wasim's.

"Come on, old son. What's up?"

Wasim's eyes misted up behind his glasses and he mumbled something.

Mr Holloway wouldn't get it. He was a nice old boy, but . . . but he was . . . well, he was white.

"What? That mumbling's no good to me, old son."

So Wasim told him.

"The 'situation'," he mumbled

"What d'yer mean, 'the situation'?

Trouble at school? Detention? Lines? What situation?"

"London. That explosion," Wasim said. "Now they don't like us."

"Us?"

Mr Holloway pointed to his chest under a shirt so big that it could have made a sail for a ship.

"Us?"

"No. . ." Wasim whispered. "Us Muslims."

"Oh, that *us*," said Mr Holloway. "D'you know what? I thought you meant the *us* that live up this street. All of *us* – you, me, your mum and dad, Mrs Smith at number thirty-five, Wally Rainer next door, old moany-britches downstairs – that *us*. . . Or you could have meant the *us* that support the Wanderers. . . There are lots of *us*es about."

He was being silly, wasn't he? And Wasim wasn't in the mood for wind-ups, not this week.

"It's *us*, the Muslims. So they beat up my brother and throw bricks and fireworks at our mosque. . ."

Mr Holloway slurped his tea and his red wrinkly eyes suddenly burned the blue of the sea again, and just that bit of him looked young enough and strong enough to lift up the Titanic. He grabbed Wasim's wrist so hard it hurt. But he didn't mean it to. He was cross.

"Listen, son. There's always a *them* and *us*. You don't need to take it personal." Suddenly he smiled. "Now, during the war. . ."

Wasim smiled to himself. You never got a Mr Holloway cup of tea without a "When I was at sea. . ." or a biscuit without a "during the war. . ." story. Mr Holloway knew they laughed at him so he said it even more slowly and loudly, and pretended to put on a sly sideways look.

"During the war. . ." Mr Holloway put on his look. "Us young 'uns got evacuated, moved out, sent out of town to escape the Blitz. All our class – Form 3B from Woodhill Infants and Juniors."

Wasim had done a topic about Britain in the 1940s so he remembered the brown-coloured photographs of kids in raincoats with boxes round their necks, and a kneeling mum at a railway station. Mr Holloway was back there now as he told his story. Wasim climbed back onto the railing balcony and helped himself to another biscuit.

"Well, we got down there, didn't we, down the country, off the train. 'Poor little lambs,' we thought they'd say, after all we'd been through. No chance. Talk about *them* and *us*. They hated us.

"We got sent to their pub to be picked for the homes we would stay in. I got picked by some couple who had a kid, Terry, a year older than me." Mr Holloway gave a not-funny laugh. "I had to share a room with him. He hated me. Wouldn't let me touch his toys or his towel, nicked my covers at night.

"It was the same in their little school the next day. Them on one side of the room – 'turnip munchers', we called 'em – and us on the other. . .

"Playtime? Fight time, more like. You got paired off – I was up against Terry. Hit me before I was ready and down I went.

"Anyway, this went on for the first week, fights everyday. Then, on the second Sunday, our mums came down and the vicar took us all down to the playing fields. 'The Friendship Footer Match', he called it. The 'smokies' – that was us – were going to play the 'turnip munchers'.

"Gawd, it got rough. Friendship? Forget it! Anyway, you wouldn't know how heavy a football was in them days, and covered in mud it was like a cannon ball.

"So the ball came to me. *Whack!* I hit it

right up Terry's jacksie – his bottom, to you,
Wasim."

The old man's eyes had lost that anger,
they'd lost the blue. They were red and
watering with tears of laughter. His belly
shook, he couldn't speak, and when he did
his voice had gone as high as a little boy's.

"He . . . he. . ." More wheezing and laughing. "He nearly took off. Could have flown up and joined the bombers going over London. *Whoosh!* it went . . . straight up his jacksie!"

The old man chortled away and Wasim, who hadn't understood half of the story, couldn't help himself and found he was giggling too.

⊙ ⊙ ⊙

"Wasim!" It was Dad shouting, and he sounded worried. "Wasim!"

Wasim waved down and Dad – who had now reached their football garage with Uncle Zan – looked very relieved.

Mr Holloway gave a cheerful wave and Dad waved back.

"Just boring him with my stories."

"Oh, that's OK. The boys love to visit you. But tonight we were worried. . ."

Mr Holloway nodded that he understood.

"Off you go, son," he said. "But hey, Wasim. . . *Them* and *us*. . . Don't take it personal. People will always make a *them* and *us*. All that about the war, when I was a boy. . . The point is, our dads were at war and a thousand planes a night were coming over to knock the stuffing out of our country so that Adolf Hitler's army could just stroll in and take over. . .

"But who became the enemy? The outsiders. Us 'smokies'. They hated us worse than they hated Hitler . . . or so it seemed to us. Cos we were a bit different, and we hadn't been there as long as them."

Wasim climbed over the balcony and on

to the garage. He gave a wave and started his balancing walk along the edge of the garages. And then he stopped.

"So, who won?"

Mr Holloway was gathering up the mugs. "What? The war?"

"No, the football. Turnips v smokies."

Mr Holloway started laughing again.

"D'you know what, son? I can't remember. And anyway, the vicar mixed the sides up for the second half. And—" The old man creased up with laughter as he remembered. "That was it. He was on my side when I did it, Terry, playing just in front of me when I got the ball. Right up his jacksie! He went up like Apollo blinkin' Thirteen!"

And Mr Holloway laughed so much that when Wasim finally jumped down, he found

Dad and Uncle Zan laughing too.

"So, what was that all about?" asked
Uncle Zan, with his kind hands on Wasim's
shoulder. And Wasim told him as they walked
– all about the smokies and the turnips, and
the *them* and *us*.

And there was a glint in Unce Zan's eye
as Wasim talked, and especially as they all
turned and gave a last wave to Mr Holloway.

"Right up his jacksie!" came a distant
shout and hoot of an eighty-year-old's little
boy laugh.

Chapter Five

Who got the toy in the cereal box? Who got
the most football cards? Who got the remote
for the telly? Who was making the other one
do all the work when they did their jobs?
Who got to sit in the front when they went
anywhere in the car?

Wasim shared a thousand arguments
every day with his brother. He also shared his
bedroom, his house, his mum, dad and sister.

He shared the garages for football and the back alley for cricket.

This morning he shared whatever it was that Atif must be feeling. He was at the door. His mates wouldn't be coming for him and he would be going into danger. Alone.

That was the 'situation' since people had begun picking sides. Not based on how good you were, like being lined up for first dibs for playground footie, but on how dark your skin was and where you said your prayers.

Now Wasim watched his brother having a last secret glance at his mobile to see if his old mates had texted, and then saw his deep breath as he opened the door and went out alone. He didn't see Mum and Dad's secret glance and Dad follow him out, because Wasim had already gone. He was with his brother. He was his team today.

At least one good thing seemed to be
happening. At school they weren't
leaving everything to him. Wasim saw that
Gary Raynor had a Soccer Sixes entry form
and was going around asking for players.
With all the fuss at home and the worry
about Atif and his school, Wasim hadn't
even bothered him with not getting a team
together, and with what would happen if
Dave and Andy didn't play. Wasim would
sort it out at dinner time.

But he didn't. The 'situation' took over
again. Wednesday was a half day at the
High School. The children there had different
hours from Wasim's school. They stayed later
than most schools all week, but then they
had Wednesday afternoon off for sports

or doing homework.

But the gathering at the playground fence, spitting and ignoring Mrs Smart, the dinner lady, didn't look like it had any homework in mind at all. They were chucking mud bombs over, and when Ben sent the ball flying over the fence, it was theirs and they started knocking it about with no intention of listening to Mrs Smart asking them nicely.

Then the High School crowd got bigger. Five or so Year Sevens and Eights became fifteen, the faces thinner and the bodies taller. The shouting voices were deeper and the sneers nastier. This was getting to be more than Mrs Smart could sort out by telling them that she knew their mums. She started telling the footballers to move back from the fence, but only a few listened and she walked, and then fast-walked and then waddle-ran up the steps and into the school building.

Nobody was interested in getting the ball back now. The bolder Year Sixes were pressed up against the wire of the fence, watching the numbers grow and smiling at the words of a chant that a few voices had started and then others had joined. Wasim had been first at the fence to get the ball back and he joined in the smiles and even started

to join the chanting like the Year Six lads
were doing.

"Oh, aye, lets go dashing,

We'll go *something* bashing."

He laughed along with the other older
kids all around him, until they sang it again
and he realised that the *something* was the
P word. . . And that it was about fighting
and beating people up.

Then he realised that all of the crowd
that had walked down from the High School
were white, and he also realised, while he was
pushing his way back through the crowd, that
his friends from his own school were still
singing, even though they looked a bit
embarrassed doing it.

Mrs Smart had made good time and
Mr Abbott was on his way down the steps
with his whistle in his mouth. He blasted it,

but nobody took any notice, because now round the corner came more navy blue jackets from the High School.

But this time the people wearing them had dark skin and they were shouting just as loudly and walking just as fast.

The white faces pulled away from the fence and Mr Abbott's whistle went mad sending his school indoors. They all wanted a last look to see what was going to happen.

Wasim looked harder than anyone else because he wanted to see if Atif was one of the brown faces that was lining up underneath the big school sign that said 'Working together, growing together'.

"Come on, Wasim, there's nothing to see here," lied Mr Abbott, almost pushing him towards the building.

But Wasim wasn't last. There was

Gary Raynor. And he was looking at his brother, Lee Raynor, the owner of the loudest voice by the fence.

"Oh, aye, let's go dashing. . ."

And Lee was looking right at Wasim.

⊙ ⊙ ⊙

Concentrating in class wasn't what Wasim was best at, anyway, but with blue lights flashing in the playground and a distant voice on a loudspeaker talking about calming down, there was no chance of Wasim reading up to page fifteen as it said to in his reading record book.

Even Mrs Johns, the classroom assistant, was looking out of the window, and Mrs Scott was only pretending to focus on her guided reading group.

"It must be kicking off out there," said Mrs Johns, and she got a look from Mrs Scott that was worse than one of the children would have been given.

Mrs Scott closed the blinds with another stare at Mrs Johns. Talk of 'kicking off' reminded Wasim about the football. He'd lost the form again and today was Wednesday –

trouble outside or not, that form and that team had to be in.

He looked around and hissed to Charles, "Soccer Sixes form. . ."

Charles just lifted his shoulders in a shrug and carried on reading. That was strange – him reading instead of thinking about football. Wasim couldn't risk getting caught because of football again, so he ticked that he'd finished his book and got up to swap.

"Miss, I've finished it, Miss. I'm swapping."

"I hope that you can tell us all about it, young man."

"Miss. . ." Wasim probably could. He'd had the same book, *The Golden Key,* in Year Three and Year Four, and he knew it off by heart. But he needed to get over to the book corner and see if someone else had a form he could fill in.

"Hmm." He pretended to be interested in *A Treasure Trove of Poems* and saw that Gary was doing the same as him – he was pretending to put his name onto his reading record book, but when Mrs Scott turned back to her guided readers he was putting names onto the Soccer Sixes entry form and colouring in the kit diagram.

Wasim relaxed. Now Charles was filling in his name and the sheet was on its way to his table. He picked up his book and started back.

Mrs Scott turned round and the sheet disappeared under Charles's desk.

"So, what did you choose, Wasim?"

"A book about pirates, Miss. . . Treasure and things. . ."

"Miss, it's poems." Donna was telling on him. "*A Treasure Trove of Poems.*"

Wasim sent her a glare. Trust Donna to show him up.

"Wasim, go to your proper blue bookshelf and choose a proper reading book."

"But. . ."

Wasim watched the Soccer Sixes entry form disappear back into Charles's tray and

made his way out of the class, and down to
the blue shelves in the corridor.

They weren't really blue. The books just
had blue stickers on and Wasim had read
most of them. But he wasn't allowed onto
the greens yet, so blues it had to be.

There were three copies of *The Golden Key*
there. He picked it again. Easy. He could read
it out loud and nobody would know that
reading in a language he didn't even speak
with his mum was hard.

And then he tiptoed past Mr Abbot's
office to try to get a look outside.

He knew he shouldn't have risked it.
The second that he passed the office door
and was in a part of the school that children
weren't allowed to be in, the front door
swung open and there was a gathering of
serious people in suits: Mr Abbott, who held

open the door for a policeman carrying a flat cap, Mrs . . . (Wasim couldn't remember her name, but she was the Headteacher of Atif's High School), another man in a dark suit and – in a grey kameez under his smart jacket – Uncle Zan!

Uncle Zan?

"Go!"

It was a bark from Mr Abbott. And Wasim went! He was back in class and reading *The Golden Key* again before he even took another breath.

Uncle Zan?

⊙ ⊙ ⊙

Afternoon play was cancelled so it was Connect Four, finishing off stories, a literacy sheet about words to describe an iceberg and flicking bits of paper at the back of your Maths book and pretending it was a goal. Wasim hadn't finished the iceberg sheet, but he was more bothered about the entry form still in Charles's tray.

Wasim burrowed deep into his pencil case and came out with the two pound coins that he needed. One for him and one for Atif.

He sauntered over to Red Group's table, where Gary and Charles were busily colouring in the team shorts and socks. Wasim dived onto the table and slid to a skilful halt just where the main colouring was going on.

"Watch it, Ahmed. You nearly jogged me."

"Soz. Got our quids."

"What for?"

"Me and Atif. Rock Star Rovers. . ."

It went quiet. And Wasim suddenly felt that Red Table was enemy territory.

"Wasim Ahmed! Are you in bed?" It was Miss Pollitt, doing the indoor play rounds.

"No, Miss."

And Wasim raised himself up and slid off the table in silence. He didn't know if his face was burning and his throat was dry because of being told off . . . or because he might not be the quickest reader in the class, but he had made out the name *Rock Star Whites* instead of *Rock Star Rovers* and he would easily have been able to read *Wasim* and *Atif*. . . But they weren't on that team sheet.

⊙ ⊙ ⊙

"His dad said," was all Charles could shrug.
"It wasn't up to me. He had to choose . . .
different mates. And Gary's dad was giving
them . . . us . . . white T-shirts, so they
changed the name."

But Wasim had walked off. The new
name had nothing to do with the shirts.

Them and *us*. . . Even Charles. He
wouldn't have started it, but it was still *them*
and *us*. Just like Mr Holloway said, only at
least Mr Holloway had got to play in a match!

There was more *them* and *us* after school.
There was a policeman standing outside the
school. There was mud and litter and a
broken bit of fence. And there were cars
everywhere. Nobody was walking home.

Wasim was especially surprised when the

policeman came straight for him and walked with him until they met Mum and Shamaila coming round from Class One and Dad coming right up the school drive to pick them up.

"Go home," somebody shouted.

"We are going home," said Shamaila.

Mum smiled a sad smile. "Yes, we are going home," she said in English. And that was strange because when it was just them she normally spoke in Urdu.

Chapter Six

It was Saturday and Wasim was in his kameez
instead of his uniform. He'd been to the
mosque with the policeman outside. He'd
done his jobs at home, he'd watched Saturday
telly but now it was back to school. It was the
Fun Day and Wasim was in charge of the
Roll the Penny game with Sally from
Year Six.

Everybody had to do something. The
Fun Day had suddenly become much more

important. Now somebody famous was going to cut the ribbon to open it and so they were expecting big crowds.

Wasim wasn't in the football so he was going to be watching pennies roll down a plank with holes in it instead. He waited by the door.

As usual since 'the situation', they were going in the car. Shamaila was really excited because she thought that they were going to a real fair, with big wheels and rides.

Atif was going because he was in a team – one with players from his school only.

Wasim looked sadly at his shin pads by the front door and climbed in to the car. He had been looking forward to today for weeks, and now it was this . . . a plank and some pennies.

It had been chaos outside school all week.

Everybody wanted to pick their children up since the High School fight outside the fence on Wednesday, and now there was a new name for 'the situation'. Now it was called 'Community Tension'. That was just a flashy way of saying *them* and *us*, Atif had explained to him through his fat lip.

But the tension at the moment was how to park cars and get into the school instead of out of it. It was madness. Cars were parked up pavements on both sides of the road. There was already a line stretching right down to the end of the school road, and once you got anywhere near the gates there were people pushing and shoving and holding tickets up in the air.

It was like when Dad had taken them to see Wanderers against Spurs in the FA Cup. There was a police van there, too, and

policemen walking about pretending to be in a Fun Day sort of mood, while Welephant, the fire brigade's mascot, walked along the line shaking hands with people.

Dad was going to drop them off and then walk back, since there was nowhere to park, so they got out just in front of a brand new sign wired to the fence.

Fun Day! GRAND OPENING
BY WORLD FAMOUS CELEBRITY - 2 PM

"Wow! Who have they got opening it?"

"Dunno," said Wasim

"Well, I'm not going to miss it, so hurry up." And Dad shooed them out.

Mum, Shamaila and Atif joined the queue and Wasim was allowed through to go to set up the Roll the Penny stall.

He walked slowly across the netball court, which was where the football was going to be played, and kicked a pebble into the real five-a-side goal net that the school had borrowed for the day.

Sally, a great big girl from Year Six, was already there and was obviously going to be in charge. Wasim wasn't bothered. Who cared about pennies dropping down holes in a plank? He doubted if whoever this world famous person was would be playing Roll the Penny.

"I bet its someone from *Corrie*," grunted Sally as she lifted up the heavy plank all by herself and rested it against the table taken from the dinner hall. She gave Wasim the job of rolling pennies down to see if the slope was right.

Wasim just breathed out and got on with

it, while the football teams arrived and started
pounding balls against the wire mesh,
juggling, heading and trying to look like
professionals.

Atif's team shuffled in and stood in
a corner passing the ball to each other.
Wasim could see his brother keeping his
head down when Dave and Andy went
past with their team.

Atif lifted his head, though, when
Lee Raynor went past. Wasim could see
him whistling at Atif's team. The crowded
playground was getting noisier but Wasim
could just about hear the tune. Where had
he heard it before?

He rolled another penny down the slope
while he thought. Wednesday. That was it. . .

Oh, aye, let's go dashing. . .

Atif's team – all of them from the
mosque – knew it too and they stopped
doing up laces and rummaging in sports bags
to stand up straight and eyeball Lee Raynor.
Raynor smiled a cocky smile and jaunted his
way, still whistling, to his team, all of them
white.

Them *and* us, thought Wasim.

When Lee's brother, Gary, and the rest of
Rock Star Rovers arrived, Wasim stopped

watching. He was glad when Sally started
bossing him about again and gave him
something to do.

The playground was filling up very
quickly. There came a whistling hoot that
had everybody holding their ears. It was
the loudspeaker hanging from the fence,
and there were lots of *ssshhhes* before
it all went silent.

"Ladies anderrrr gentlemen. . ."

There was a surge towards the fence and
the sight of a long, white stretch limousine
that seemed to be the length of the school
road.

It was the star coming to open the fair . . .
in a stretch limo! Wasim forgot himself and
joined the running children and fast-walking
adults trying to get as near to the gate as they
could.

Wasim wasn't bothered about the Fun Day now that he wasn't in a team, but even he wanted to know who this famous person was. He tried to think of all the famous people he knew. It must be the queen to have a limo that long.

"I told you, Waz! It's the queen. . . Has to be in a stretch limo like that." Charles was proud of himself, until a glare from Lee Raynor – now with football shorts under his black hoodie top – cut him down. Charles shot Wasim an *I'm sorry* look and stood back on tiptoe trying to gaze into the tinted windows of the million-mile car.

Wasim's chest felt heavy again. Obviously Rock Star Whites weren't even supposed to talk to people like Wasim, let alone pick them for the same team. It was a nothing sort of feeling – like saying goodbye to Grandma at the airport when she went back to Pakistan and knowing he wouldn't see her for ages. Sad. Just sad.

The limo came to a halt and some people started cheering and clapping. The whistling in the speakers came again and then there was a crackle and a click – a CD going on – and everyone waited for the music.

"God Save the Queen, I bet," said Wasim to Sally, who was the only person he knew in his bit of the crush. She just wrinkled her eyebrows and looked at him.

Another crackle and the music crashed through the old school speakers.

BAM! BAM, BAM, BAM. . . BAM, BAM, BAM. . . BAMMMM!

"*Rocky*!"

It was Atif, who had pushed through next to him and was boxing. And everyone else seemed to know the tune, too, because they were all punching into the air in time to each BAM. Charles was air-punching but he looked puzzled and Sally shouted, "Not quite God Save the Queen. I don't think she's into boxing."

"So?" Wasim said. "She might be. . ." he added, and then looked around, hoping nobody had heard him.

BAM! BAM, BAM, BAM. . .

There was another crackle and the music went off. Then came the strange, deep voice again, speaking – like they did on WW wrestling or boxing on the TV – in an American accent with the end of each word stretched out as long as the limo that everybody was crowding to stare into.

"Ladeeeezzzz anderrr gentlemen, boyzzz anderrrr girlzzzz."

It all went quiet and there was a big
sucking in of breath as, just like a space ship,
the back door of the limo suddenly hissed
and moved a few centimetres all on its own.
It was opening!

The *Rocky* music took over again.

BAM! BAM! BAMMMMMMM!

"Pleazzzzzzzze be upstanding. . ."

Well, they all were upstanding already but
they stood even higher on their tiptoes, and
Wasim found himself hugging Atif and Sally
in his excitement. The door hissed wider and
they all strained to see into the blackness as
out stepped. . .

Uncle Zan!

Wasim and Atif just stared at each other.
Uncle Zan was in his best jacket and kameez,
with the photographer from the paper
clicking at him, and a huge disappointed suck

of breath from the playground

But Uncle Zan was smiling and shaking his head, and skipping out of the way.

BAM! BAM! BAM! BAM! BAM, BAM, BAM!

"Ladeezzzz and gentlemen. Be upstanding forrr . . . theeeeee Olympic gold medal winner, THE three times Golden Glove winner and . . . now . . . THEEE undisputederr Middle Weight Boxing Champion of the worlderrrr. . . Our town's very own. . ."

BAM, BAM, BAMMM!

". . . Sayidddddd Aaaaaaakram!"

And out he came!

BAM! BAM! BAM!

Bouncing on his golden trainers, punching into the air in a blur that was too fast to see, kissing his golden gloves and

jogging on the spot
in pure white
dressing gown with
golden writing that
read *Sayid*.

Sayid Akram . . .
the Champ!

The screams,
whistles and cheers
drowned out *Rocky*
on the loudspeaker.
It really was Sayid
Akram, the World
Champ, and the
most famous person
that had ever been born in the town.

He'd learned his trade at the boxing club
near here, and he'd come back from the
Olympics with his gold medal to this town,

and he'd returned from America, the World
Champion and loved by everyone, to this
town.

He was a local boy. He'd gone to school
around here. He went to a mosque around
here. Sayid Akram. Everybody's son,
everybody's brother, everybody's friend.
Everybody loved Sayid and. . .

Wasim turned and shared a glance with
his real brother. And he was a Muslim.
He was from round here and he was a
Muslim . . . just like Wasim and Atif.

For the first time since he'd come home
battered and bruised, there was a gleam in
Atif's eyes. And Wasim thought that there
was probably the same gleam in his own.
It was pride. Sayid Akram belonged to
everybody, but most of all, Wasim felt,
he belonged to him.

Wasim hugged his brother again and his shining eyes went over his shoulder to where everybody was still fist-pumping to the *Bam Bam Bams* of *Rocky*.

And then his eyes caught two more. Lee Raynor's. But not for long. Because Lee Raynor's eyes, that had blazed and hated outside the mosque and by the fence, dropped down and looked closely at the concrete of the playground. And Wasim knew why.

Sayid Akram. The Champ!

Chapter Seven

Next to *The Golden Key* on the blue shelves
at school was a book called *The Pied Piper of
Hamelin*. Wasim hadn't read it yet, but he had
seen the coloured picture on the front. It was
of hundreds of kids following a man who
was blowing on a recorder or something.

That was what it was like as Sayid, the
Champ, made his way around the stalls of
the fair, pretending to have a go at each thing.

The big man who walked around in front of Sayid wouldn't let anyone shake his hand. It was in case they broke it, Sally said.

Wasim had stayed up to watch Sayid win his World Championship belt a few months ago and he'd seen what that hand could do, so he was surprised that he would worry about kids from their school breaking it, but nobody argued.

They just followed him, screaming his name and trying to get photos on their mobile phones of each other pretending to punch the Champ. Even Wasim's dad got one!

Then the procession turned from the
Hook a Duck paddling pool and headed
to Roll the Penny. Wasim couldn't swallow.
He tried to look cool as he found himself
standing to attention at the table where his
pile of pennies were waiting to be rolled.

"This is my nephew, Wasim." Wasim
fought for breath. The Champ's minder had
stood to one side when Uncle Zan spoke and
now Sayid Akram – Sayid from the Olympics,
Sayid from the papers, Sayid from the Corn
Puffs advert – came up to him.

"How you doing, man?" asked the
Champion of the World.

It had been a special treat for Wasim and
Atif when Sayid had fought his boxing match
to become World Champ. It wasn't on
normal telly but Dad had driven Wasim
and Atif to one of his friend's houses to

watch it on Pay-per-view at two o' clock in the morning!

That night in Las Vegas, America, Sayid had danced around the ring to crashing music just like he did today, and a voice had boomed his name with a *Ladeezz and err gentlemennn*, just like today. Sayid had been brilliant, dancing all over the ring, and punching in a blur of red gloves and then skipping away before he could be touched by the bigger boxer he was fighting.

Afterwards, he'd been interviewed holding a massive belt – out of breath and sweating, but grinning underneath swollen cheeks and a puffy eye.

Now Wasim was right next to that person. He had never been near to anyone from the TV before and it was strange. Sayid looked small in the ring next to some of the other boxers, but here he looked massive. The skin that had been sweating and bruised after the big fight was smooth and glowing with fitness, and as Sayid leaned over to pick up a penny, Wasim could actually sense specialness.

Even though he was only going to roll a penny, you could somehow tell that this wasn't an ordinary person, this was someone who was actually the best in the whole world at what he did. Every movement was relaxed and unhurried, but underneath the white tracksuit top and a massive gold chain, hard shoulder muscles rippled up to a neck like a tree trunk.

And *he* wanted to know how Wasim was doing!

Sayid gave Wasim a pretend punch on the arm and then rolled the penny. He got a

massive cheer, did a World Champ's shake
of his fists and dance, and before Wasim
could even say how he was really doing,
the great crowd moved off.

Wasim carried on feeling pleased until he saw that the Champ was heading to the Super Sixes, the football. And Wasim wasn't in it. He looked over to the Raynors and Charles, the new Rock Star Rovers, Rock Star *Whites*, and rubbed his arm where the Champ had hit him. But it wasn't his arm that was hurting.

◉ ◉ ◉

The Woodley Wanderers would have been pleased with a crowd that big. There they all were, gathered around the netball court – which was now a mini football pitch – watching two teams ready to play the first match of the Soccer Sixes tournament. Rock Star Whites v AC Wizards – Atif's team.

But what a tournament! Because, in the

middle, instead of Mr Abbott with his suit trousers tucked into his socks and a playtime whistle, there was a proper referee and next to him – the World Champ.

"Ladeezzz anderrr gentlemenner. . . Anderr now . . . the main event. . . To kick off our Soccer Sixes competitionnerr . . . in the green corner. . ."

Off came Sayid's brilliant white and gold trackie top and underneath was an emerald green football shirt. The exact colour of the Pakistan flag.

"In the green corner . . . the undefeated World Champion and now centre-forward, Mr Sayiiiiiiiid Akkkkkkkram!"

The noise was now deafening and, even though he had promised himself that he wouldn't even watch, Wasim found himself dragged over to the pitch by the commotion.

Sayid did his dance again round the pitch. He high-fived the players who were all ready to go and couldn't believe they were on the pitch with Sayid Akram, with hundreds of people squashed round.

Wasim squeezed his way through and he could see that his brother was having the same trouble he sometimes had. He couldn't keep the smile from spreading all over his bruised face. Sayid was going to kick off for them against Rock Star Whites. Against Lee Raynor's team.

Sayid touched his toes, jumped on the spot and then the crowd roared as he got down and did ten press ups on one arm, clapping his hands in the middle of each one, and then did ten on the other arm. Then he used his arms to flip himself up in the air, ready to start.

Wasim looked over at Rock Star Whites and he was pleased – they weren't smiling. Least of all Lee Raynor. He was looking very worried and had moved back from the kick-off spot. He was now back as far from Atif's team and Sayid Akram as the netball court would allow. He was whispering to the goalkeeper – another familiar face, Jason Coolley. Wasim thought back to the terror outside his mosque last week, the smell of the firework and the hating face shouting at his family when they got out.

"It's not fair!" was all the owner of the face managed this time. "Him playing for them. He'll. . . It's not fair."

But nobody was listening. And Jason Coolley and Lee Raynor looked very thin and very white and very scared as Sayid bounced the ball ready to start.

The ref blasted his whistle and Sayid made a big joke of getting a brand new leather ball out of his bag and hiding it behind his back until the ref wagged a jokey finger at him and made him put it down. Everybody laughed.

Then Sayid tapped the ref on the arm and signalled him to wait. He picked up the bag and slowly looked up at Rock Star Whites. Then the Champ fixed them with the Akram stare and made a step towards them.

For the first time that afternoon it went silent. Completely silent. He wouldn't . . . would he?

And then the World Champ shook hands with the team at his end – the team of Muslims – and he marched towards Rock Star *Whites*.

Chapter Eight

At their school, if a grown-up said, "Stop and listen!" everyone had to fold their arms and stop talking. That was just what it was like when Sayid Akram shook hands with the AC Wizards and marched at Rock Star Whites. Two hundred people, probably more than that, and they'd all gone as quiet as when somebody got told off in assembly.

It was a walk that they'd all seen before.

Not the walk to get his Sports Personality of the Year award, or the walk to get his gold medal at the Olympics.

No. This was the walk he did towards the boxing ring. The walk into battle before those minutes when he had to go out there and earn the stretch limos and the gold chains and all this cheering. When he had to go and get punched by the best in the world. Not the best in a class, or the toughest in the school, but the best fighters in the *world*.

The walk when Sayid, everybody's son and everybody's brother, had to go out and be the best in the world against men who, just like him, had spent their whole lives becoming fighting machines.

This walk wasn't about legs that could dodge and skip and bounce, or arms like metal springs that moved so fast you had to wait for the slow motion replay to see them.

This was a walk that came from the eyes. And those eyes had hushed the crowd around the pitch. They had Lee Raynor walking backwards and the rest of Rock Star Whites looking for their mums. The World Champion was coming for them.

Wasim took his eyes off of the Champ to look over at his brother again. This was what he'd wanted ever since he'd seen the firework come into the mosque and the fingers sticking up on the bus, and especially after he'd seen Atif's battered face during the week.

He hadn't caused any explosions and everyone he knew was sickened by the sort of people that had. So what had happened since – the fighting and the name-calling and the being left out – was not fair! And now here was someone to stick up for them.

But it was just like when he'd had the chance to send a Wasim rocket shot against Robert Bailey in his Woodley Wanderers trial. Suddenly, Wasim wasn't sure he wanted it.

⊙ ⊙ ⊙

The walk only lasted seconds, and so did the silence, because suddenly – *WHACK!* – Sayid sent the duffle bag he was carrying thundering into the ground. The fighter's eyes burned one more flame and then, quick as the punches that made him the best in the world, his arms shot into the bag.

"You! You! You!"

And out came the silky green Nike football shirts like the one that he was wearing. He threw them at Rock Star

Whites – one each.

"Yours, yours, yours. Hurry up, lads. It's showtime! I'm up front."

And Sayid set the ball on the centre spot and leaned over the ref. He gave him a kiss on top of his bald head and blew the whistle hanging round his neck. The crowd howled with laughter and roared as Sayid passed the ball to Charles, who was still putting his shirt on but managed to get it back to him. Then the Champ took the ball around Faizhan and hammered a shot at goal. The shot hit Atif on the chest, but he managed to get the ball down to his feet and clear it.

And that was it. It was football now and everything else forgotten.

◉ ◉ ◉

The Champ had done his bit by then. He did

a few juggles to get a laugh but actually, he might have been the best in the world at boxing, but he definitely wasn't the best at football.

After a few minutes he went into a tackle and pretended to be fouled and rolled over and over to get more cheers and pretend jeers.

"OK, OK," he clowned, "I give up. You guys are too tough for me. . ." And, pretending to be out of breath and limping, he made his way to the side.

Everyone knew that he was joking and that he had been a really good sport. They cheered and clapped him off.

But one voice shouted louder than the others. It was Khaled, who Wasim had seen leading a group down to the playground when it had 'kicked off' outside school.

"Hey, Sayid!" he shouted. "How come you played for them – for the Whites?"

Then Sayid Akram's eyes flashed again and he turned back to the pitch to face the shout. It was silent again.

"I didn't," the Champ grinned. "I played for the Greens."

There was silence. Then one clap. Then two. Then everyone was clapping. They all got it. The Champ had broken the *them* and *us*.

Wasim felt an arm round his shoulder. It was Uncle Zan, with Mr Holloway next to him, slurping away at a cup of tea.

"What do you think of that, Wasim? Just like Mr Holloway's story. A football match to bring people together. I know Sayid's dad from his mosque. He's a real champ, yes?"

Wasim nodded slowly. And then he was
nodding some more – Sayid was talking
to him.

"OK, mate. Can you sub for me?"

Wasim couldn't stop nodding. The World
Champ was pulling off his green football
shirt and handing it over. Wasim just stared.

"You'd better get on there, mate."

And Wasim found himself in a proper
World Champ's Nike football shirt running
on to play for Rock Star— To play for the
Greens! And it turned out that it was *against*
the Whites. Because, from another bag,
Sayid had produced a set of proper white
Wanderers shirts, real ones, just like they
sold in the club shop. And he had given
them to the AC Wizards.

Wasim looked around at his teammates.
His excitement turned to nervousness.
But it had been OK for a World Champ
Muslim to play for the Greens, so now it
had to be OK for a Year Five Muslim to
play for them. This wasn't black and white, or
Asian and English. It was coming together –
green shirts against white ones. So it wasn't
about winning. . .

But Wasim Ahmed was Wasim Ahmed

and he always tried to win, and, whatever they were thinking, he was there to help the Greens out. So, soon he was crunching into tackles against Atif, Faizhan and the others.

Then Gary Raynor got the ball on the centre spot. Wasim called for it and the ball came. He went round one, two and *BLAST!* The ball hit the back of the five-a-side net and rocked it backwards.

The crowd were all still there, and there was a roar they could have heard in Las Vegas.

⊙ ⊙ ⊙

That should have been the best bit. But it wasn't!

Wasim's massive green shirt was

everywhere – the cheers seemed to have
given him ten sets of lungs. And then he got
the ball at the back and was ready to start a
new attack. The rest of the green shirts had
moved up, ready, and were calling for the ball.

Except for one of them. It was
Lee Raynor. He was a smoker already, and
now he was wheezing and bending down
with his hands on his knees.

Wasim glanced up to pass and he could
see Mr Holloway in his cap and blue blazer,
and huge trousers pulled almost up to his
chest by his red braces. Wasim looked up
one more time and it could have been his
imagination, but he was sure Mr Holloway
was mouthing something to him from
behind his plastic cup. What was it?

And then Wasim caught sight of
Lee Raynor bending over and he worked out

what the old man was saying.

"Right up his jacksie!"

And Wasim hit it.

That was the best bit!

ALSO AVAILABLE:

Wasim the Wanderer
(selected for Boys into Books 5-11)

Wasim One Star
(A Scholastic Best Book of the Year)

Wasim's Challenge
(shortlisted for the Coventry Inspiration Awards)

Praise for other *Wasim* titles:

"A character that primary school
children and teachers will recognise
and respond to with pleasure."

Guardian

"Ashley has a lively style with ... contemporary
vocabulary. Full of everyday action and humour."

Books for Keeps

CHRIS ASHLEY

One of Chris Ashley's greatest heroes was a boxer,
Mohammed Ali. He won an Olympic gold medal for
his country and the day he arrived home wearing it
around his neck, he was not allowed to buy
a hamburger in his home town ... because
he was black. It was *them* and *us*.

But Ali was such a brilliant boxer, as well as a
fantastic character, that just a few years later the
whole world was cheering him on. It was just *us*
when Ali was boxing, people forgot everything
except that he was "The Greatest".

It's just *us* in most schools that Chris knows.
Children aren't like some grown-ups, they like things
to be fair, so they choose their friends based on
what they are like and what they can do.
Nothing else matters.

Chris has two wishes. He wishes grown-ups all
around the world could learn from children.
And he wishes he could have met Mohammed Ali.
The Greatest!

Read more about
Wasim's adventures!

Wasim the Wanderer

Chris Ashley
Illustrated by Kate Pankhurst

No one at school can score a goal like Wasim!
So he is trying out his football skills for
Teamwork 10,000 and that might just lead
to a trial with the Woodley Wanderers! But how
can he play his best football with Robert Bailey
lurking around every corner – and then
on the football pitch too?

Wasim One Star

Chris Ashley
Illustrated by Kate Pankhurst

Wasim wants to be a One-Star swimmer.
But when the day comes to take the plunge,
Wasim's up to his neck in trouble. When Wasim
gets ordered out of the pool for talking to the
new boy, Wayne, his chances of getting his One Star
vanish. Will Wasim be a star or must he wait
until next year for his chance to shine?

WASIM'S CHALLENGE

Chris Ashley
Illustrated by Kate Pankhurst

Wasim's class are off to Snowdonia on a
Challenge by Choice week and he can't wait!
And that's not the only challenge Wasim is facing –
this year he has secretly decided to fast
for Ramadan for the first time.
But as usual, nothing goes right for Wasim,
and when a box of Mars bars disappears,
he becomes prime suspect. Can he prove
his innocence and complete his challenges?

SITA, SNAKE-QUEEN OF SPEED

Franzeska G. Ewart

When Yosser's best friend, Kylie, comes back from
Thrill City she is full of amazing stories about
the best ride there – Sita, Snake-Queen of Speed!
Yosser knows that she MUST go on the ride…
but how? An opportunity presents itself when
Kylie's dad's prize ferret, Thunderball Silver the Third,
mysteriously goes missing just days before
the Grand Ferret Championships.
Will Yosser and Kylie fid a way to catch
the ferret-thief and earn enough money
to make their dreams come true?